A Rosie and Rasmus STORY

Where the Dragons Live

written and illustrated by
SERENA GEDDES

ALADDIN

New York   London   Toronto   Sydney   New Delhi

ALADDIN

An imprint of Simon & Schuster Children's Publishing Division

1230 Avenue of the Americas, New York, New York 10020

First Aladdin hardcover edition July 2020

Copyright © 2020 by Serena Geddes

For information about special discounts for bulk purchases, please contact

Simon & Schuster Special Sales at 1-866-506-1949 or business@simonandschuster.com.

The Simon & Schuster Speakers Bureau can bring authors to your live event. For more

information or to book an event contact the Simon & Schuster Speakers Bureau

at 1-866-248-3049 or visit our website at www.simonspeakers.com.

Designed by Laura Lyn DiSiena

The illustrations for this book were rendered in watercolor.

The text of this book was set in Janson and Quimbly.

Manufactured in China 0420 SCP

10 9 8 7 6 5 4 3 2 1

Library of Congress Control Number 2019912397

ISBN 978-1-4814-9876-0 (hc)

ISBN 978-1-4814-9877-7 (eBook)

This is Rasmus.

He left his friend Rosie and his
tree on the top of the hill . . .

to fly to the island where the dragons live.

The dragons kicked rocks, bared their claws,
blew fire, and roared their loudest roars.

When they stopped, Rasmus smiled,
for he had never met another dragon before.

But to all these big dragons, Rasmus was different. . . .

And they let him know.

Rasmus watched as the other dragons played.

He started to kick a rock.

He tried breathing fire,

but only gas came out.

And he practiced his roar.

But he still felt alone.

Rasmus felt sad.

Then he felt angry.

This is Rosie.

She is sailing to the island where the dragons live.

Rasmus was very happy to see his friend Rosie.

But he had some explaining to do.

Rosie and Rasmus hugged . . .

celebrated,

said hello to a new friend,

and said goodbye to a treasured one.